Pencils Made

This Scar

by Steven Saus

Alliteration Ink | Dayton

The cover artwork is a royalty-free image by and © Stuart Key, purchased from Dreamstime.com . You can find more of Stuart's work at www.stuartkey.co.uk.

Published by
Alliteration Ink
Dayton, OH 45420
alliterationink.com

Pencils Made This Scar
ISBN No. 978-0-9840065-2-6

July 2010, March 2012
10 9 8 7 6 5 4 3 2

Table of Contents

Steven Saus

Foreword

I wrote my first drabble a decade before I wrote my second.

I enjoy the challenge of drabbles and flash fiction. Tell a story in one or two hundred words. It should have character, conflict, and resolution.

Each provides a glimpse - just a glimpse - into someone else's life. But that glimpse must be *meaningful* - it must *imply* the rest of their life as well.

Do not try to sit and read this straight through. Read a story. Take a moment or three, or more. Then come back.

In this book, every page is its own story.

I hope you enjoy them.

Underwear

When I was a kid, I loved Indiana Jones.

I would walk around with my shirts unbuttoned to my pasty navel, carrying a string for a whip. I ran around the schoolyard humming the theme song.

I also loved my Luke Skywalker Underoos. When friends came over, I would sometimes show them off, coming downstairs wearing nothing but the orange underwear.

That was decades ago.

Yesterday, a friend asked me what I was going to be for Halloween.

"I don't know," I replied. But my hand fidgeted with my shirt buttons, and I swear my underwear suddenly turned bright orange.

Great-Uncle

Uncle Al smelled of vaporub as he poked at me. "How's my little girl?"

My young voice squeaked angrily at him. "I. Am. A. Boy."

Al ran his finger through his thick black hair. "Okay, little girl." He reached out, and I felt a brief tug. "Gotcher nose!"

"I'm a boy! And that's your finger, not my nose."

I smiled. "I've got one too, Uncle." I reached towards his scalp, then put my hand in my pocket. "Guess what I've got, Uncle."

He shrieked, feeling the air cold against his suddenly bald scalp.

"Oh," I said. "You figured it out."

Clubbing

She smiled - brightness slashing through the dense music of the bar, transforming him into an instant mass of cliches.

An awkward smile creased his lips, brain racing on a wave of adrenaline, considering and rejecting a thousand trite lines.

He stared at her, wondering what the best approach would be. Beads of sweat formed on his nose; his heavy glasses started to slide down his face.

They were adjusted by a nervous finger as he started to walk across the bar.

He still had no idea what he'd say. But then her lover returned, so it didn't matter anyway.

Generation Ship Zed

As a child I read illustrated books about asteroid starships. I dreamed of living in generation ships - islands of humanity in the void. And now I do.

A cylinder is our artificial sun. Fields of grains feed us and regrown our oxygen. The asteroid's spin provides gravity. Imagine a multiracial Rockwell painting in space. We'll make a new world like in the books.

The books left out the undead horde writhing over the planet we left behind. The other ships have already succumbed, signals vanishing after a few transmitted screams.

Our ship is uninfected.

But oh God, am I hungry.

Tree-Told Tales

A long time ago, Best Beloved, when the tree people returned from their vacation, they were very tired. They'd gone to the Bahamas, and it was a very long walk back.

So when the tree people got home, they wanted to sleep. But they couldn't. The mostly hairless apes that lived next door kept them up all night long. The apes were making babies really loudly.

So the next day, while the apes slept peacefully, breathing clearly, the tree people returned the favor. That night, the apes' noses were too clogged to make babies.

And the tree people slept peacefully.

Darrin 1990

"She's a half hour late."

I shrugged and gave him a sheepish look as I lounged on the porch banister. "Maybe she's stuck in traffic, man."

"It's nine at night. There's no fucking traffic."

He paced around his porch some more, smoking cigarettes one after another, flicking the butts into the street.

I jumped when he punched the other side of the old banister. "Darrin, man, calm down. She'll get here."

He pushed past me and went upstairs. The sounds of some metal band vibrated the windows, and I waited for his girlfriend, watching the cigarette cherries cool into carbon.

Fantasy Reality TV

"So Sandy," Gerard said, "you say that Kut-Haran isn't a good husband."

"He doesn't give us krat!" the female kobold screeched. The studio audience roared approval.

Gerard pointed to stage left. "Well, here he is!"

Kut-Haran was not a kobold. He was a nine foot tall troll. The studio chair broke under his weight. This episode Gerard would have to keep it calm.

"Okay, Sandy," Gerard said, but she was screeching obscenities at Kut-Haran. The crowd shouted, chanting Gerard's name. When the troll grabbed its club, Gerard buried his head in his hands.

He didn't get paid enough for this.

Inside, Outside, Upside Down

Before, there was screaming.

The screams were in my head. It was all too much. Keeping up the house. Having the newest car. The stupid forms at work. Her marathon shopping sprees. The kids deciding their new hobby was too boring after we'd rearranged our schedules. Working twelve hour days to afford it all.

Even the dog growled at me.

Then the bum bit me. Twelve hours later, and I'm infected like him. It's simple now. I hunger for human flesh, and I kill. And I eat.

The screams are outside my head now.

But my mind is at peace.

Chocolate Pudding Homecoming

The recipe amused her: "As this homey dessert bakes..." It was appropriate, in an overdone kind of way. He had been gone for just over a year. He would appreciate a little care package.

The scoop whuffed a small puff of flour onto her mother's old cookbook. When she cooked, her mother's memory was close. She could almost hear her voice.

"Sissy, get all the ingredients together before you start cooking," it chided. Fine.

Sugar. Eggs. Baking powder. Metal file. Chocolate. Vanilla.

Her son called from the other room. "Mommy, when will Daddy come home?"

"Soon, baby. Real soon."

Not Me

It's not my fault. I didn't do my schoolwork because Tommy McDonald kept flicking my neck with his pencil. Then the teacher yelled at me when I told him to stop.

And I didn't put the monster in my closet.

I crawled into bed next to Mom. She didn't wake up until Dad started yelling again. He said I was too old to be scared of monsters, and smacked me around for crying.

Mom didn't say anything. She didn't stop him.

Before I left their room, their closet door opened. A big fanged mouth smiled at me.

I smiled back.

Essay Question

She collects the fee from the nightstand. He rubs his ring finger, counting ribs as her shirt slides over them.

"I gotta run," she says. "I have a exam in biology to study for."

"I had an exam at the hospital yesterday," he blurts.

She giggles. "What grade did you get?"

He remembers the scan full of unexpected metastatic dots.

"They don't give grades." He hopes his smile seems natural.

After she leaves, he rolls upright, lights a cigarette - why stop now? - and stares at the door.

He opens the nightstand drawer, removes the book, and desperately begins to cram.

High Piracy

Smoke billowed from the ship's wreckage. Captain Saunders and his crew baked on the sun blasted island beach. In the near distance, the pirate ship sailed back out to sea.

"This is a right mess, Cap'n," his first mate said. He stroked the grey stubble of his beard. "Those pirates marooned us here, wrecked our ship, and stole all our cargo!" He stomped his boot in the sand. "And them pirates was just women!"

Captain Saunders sighed. "They stole more than our cargo, Smitty." He touched the ragged hole in his chest and smiled.

"She stole far more than that."

One

You scream over the echoes of the bomb: "Call 911!"

Two rescue breaths, just like in the book, move down. Find the xyphoid, ignore the twisted shape of his ribs and push push.

Ignore that this kid had shoved in front of you, ignore his shrapnel and his burned flesh on your hands. Push push. Move back up, head-tilt-chin-thrust.

He's young, no lines on his face, then the sirens and wounded wail in chorus, remember breathe, breathe. Fingers on his neck, feel for a pulse, feel for breath on your cheek. C'mon, any pulse.

Just a little heartbeat.

Just one.

Simple Relationships

When we dated, her lips brushed my ear, saying: "I don't want to get into anything complicated." Now, one lip hangs decomposing from her ruined face.

I stumble back over the playroom's plastic chairs. I had pretended nothing was wrong, had imagined she was happy. Our son's first birthday pictures show her flat expression and storebought birthday cake. She - it, zombies are it - drops his gnawed arm.

Trapped in the corner, I can't run from reality anymore. I level the shotgun.

"Keep it simple, baby."

I fire one barrel through my sobs and her head.

I save one barrel for me.

Saving Your Bacon

I ran as fast as my stubbly little hooves would go. Gary said my running was "higgledly-piggledly", but Gary's dead now.

My tree had fallen. It wasn't strong enough. Stronger than Gary's straw hut, strong enough to give me a chance to run, but that was all.

Ralph stared wide-eyed at me through the window of his brick house.

"Let me in!"

A tear ran down Ralph's cheek. He didn't open the door.

The wolf's breath was hot on my neck.

"Your choice, little piggy. I'll eat you any way you want."

I tried to choose something quick.

Hospital Awesome

The antiseptic hospital stink makes it through the red rubber nose. He shuffles faster, seeing her outside his son's room. His ex-wife's distinctive braid swings over a black clad shoulder, a katana across her back.

He yells over the flapping of his oversize shoes. "A ninja? In a hospital?"

"He likes ninjas!"

"That was a year ago! Clowns make everyone happy!"

He realized that wasn't true as she hit him.

Later, the police handcuffed them outside the room. Bobby beamed out, cancer forgotten at the spectacle of clowns fighting ninjas.

His real smile was far bigger than the painted one.

Moonshine

I found Maria by the airlock, avoiding hyperventilation by puffing into the sack. Her hair swirled in the spaceship's low gravity.

She gasped "It's starting!" before breathing into the paper again.

"What's starting?" I asked.

She pointed at the porthole. I looked out, into the black. "I don't see..." I said, then I did.

The moon, still dark and new from Earth's viewpoint, showed a different face to our spaceship. We saw the far side of the moon. It shone bright and full.

Maria's hand, now more of a paw, fell on my shoulder.

Behind me, I heard a growl.

Jonas and Boyd

The sea of bones pounded the gate below. Jonah looked through his helm at the mass of skeletons - all the world's dead, rallied against the kingdom - and fought the urge to piss his pants.

"We are so screwed," he muttered, fingers tightening around his swordhilt.

His shieldmate Boyd shrugged and took another drink from his flask.

"I told ya to f'in drink first." Boyd wobbled a little in bravado or drunkeness, Jonah couldn't tell. "Just gotta get in there and start swingin'."

Jonah shook his head. "How long 'till you become one of them like that?"

"Only about three seconds before you, my friend!" Boyd's smile faltered. "Only three seconds, mate."

Jonas and Boyd II

The demons came from the campfire's smoke. Jonah woke at Reyald's scream. Boyd slept until Reyald's head bounced off his stomach.

"Last time I let Reyald stand watch," Boyd grumbled, drawing his sword.

"You know," Jonah said as he parried a claw, "I think that someone wants us dead." He thrust upward, drenching himself in demon blood.

Boyd dodged a tentacle. "Nah." He stabbed the tentacle before it could grab Jonah.

"Thanks," Jonah replied, pouring holy water on a demon. "But you disagree?"

Boyd sliced open the last demon's abdomen. "Yeah." He sat down. "I think someone wanted these demons dead."

Playing Doubles

She lays in the motel bed with him, afternoon sun hot on bare skin.

Two rings lay on the nightstand. Hers is a frilly feminine one her husband chose. His is a thick, simple, plain band. He told his wife what style of ring he'd wear.

He didn't make a decision on his own after that. Not until they met.

She kisses the rough stubble on his cheek, and wakes him. She carefully does not say - refuses to say - "Time to go."

They kiss, and they dress. She will leave her ring on the nightstand, and wonders if he will.

Rocker

It first creaked as she rocked in summer's heat, waiting for the baby. Dad fixed it, but she wouldn't sit in it until he made it squeak again.

She rocked through my breastfeeding and tantrums. I showed up once with teenage bravado and a cigarette. She stopped. I put the cigarette out and heard the rhythmic creak again.

I missed it when I left for college. Squeaks lulled me to sleep when I returned for Dad's funeral.

It's silent now. My wife asks if I'm okay.

The wind moves the rocker, and for a second I pretend that I am.

Corporate Zombie

Hush. Do not say another word.

You stand out. You are not dressed like them - no suit, no power tie, no flag pin. They swarm downtown during the day. Nighttime is safer; they shelter in their homes.

I can pass among them. I can rattle off last week's scores and the contestants on the reality TV shows. You have to talk in soundbites, not analysis. Are you stupid? They will eat your brain if they notice you.

Damn. My co-workers. Follow my lead.

Bobby! Yeah, shame about last night. We were just talking about who got voted off, right?

Right?

Bartender's Guide

It wasn't supposed to be like this. The guests praise the drinks, my bartending skills. It is part of why Vinnie's parties are popular.

I used to be the bad child, "not gonna amount to nothing"; a stark contrast to my sister's channeled angel... until Vinnie took me in. A foot soldier, then lieutenant, now barkeep and "cleaner". I'd straightened up even as gambling devoured my sister's bank account, house, marriage. Her debts got out of hand. Her assets were...liquidated.

"Howdja get your Bloody Marys so good?" a mobster calls at me.

"Family secret," I say, heading towards the kitchen.

Positioning

Samantha always knew the exact location of the door. She knew the ways to exit any room. She knew when to run, when to hide, when to agree, when to be silent. These lessons were her mother's gifts.

His rampages were a time for silence.

She did not flinch as bits of smashed vase skittered across the kitchen floor. The vase was her mother's. A shard came to rest against her toe.

She looked up at him, angry in the kitchen doorway.

Samantha always knew the exact location of the door.

She also knew the exact location of the icepick.

Bless You

My roommate said he moved to Florida from Hurricane, West Virginia, though he pronounced it Hurr-eh-cun and threatened to fight me over it.

"It's where the hurricane names come from," he told me. "One at a time, we get sick. It's alphabetical, but skips around. One year boys, the next girls. As we get sicker, the storm gets worse."

"But you live here now," I said.

He shook his head. "The sickness follows us. It's where you're born that counts."

He went to bed early that night. The next day he had a fever, and clouds massed on the horizon.

Fetishes

I loved Sally, though I couldn't understand why a model like her would be with a nerd like me. I told myself I would do anything to get a girl like her.

That's why I didn't object when she squished the bug during sex. "It's what gets me off," she said.

It had been so long, I didn't care. And at first, it was a little exciting.

Then it was spiders. Centipedes. Mice. Birds. A hamster.

When it was finally my own head squeezed under her stilleto heel, I realized I didn't really love her.

It was only a crush.

Playing Dress Up

My son puts on a newsboy cap, picks up a newspaper and his voice rings out: "Extra, extra, read all about it!"

I laugh, and he tosses the hat aside. He grabs a cop's hat and waves a baton. A helmet, and he's lowcrawling along the floor.

I see the fedora, but I'm not fast enough. Steel eyes gaze from under its brim.

"Couldn't wait for the inheritance," my father says through my son.

I stumble backward as my son, wearing my father's hat and my father's eyes, raises the knife.

"You never could wait," he said.

"But I could."

Job Satisfaction

Kethin's legs squeezed against the dragon's scales as they rose into the winter night. His furs warmed him, but his eyes were freezing behind the goggles. The mountain cave fell away behind the dragon's wings. The cold moonlight shone on fleeing clouds and glittering snow below.

Kethin spotted the town lights below. He leaned forward, and the dragon dove for the city. At the last moment, he drove in his spurs and pulled up. Dragonfire lashed out, and they rose high over the street, wet with newly melted snow.

"One of these days," Kethin thought, "I'll get an interesting job."

Pretense of Snowflakes

Snowflakes float lazily as she begins shouting. I do not fight back, and this infuriates her. Crystalline water sparkles in angled sunlight, like the shining stone in her ring that bounce bounce bounces on the floor.

She leaves tire tracks in the driveway, a bit of rubber on the street. Her suitcase, her car are gone, and so is she.

Fat wet flakes fall, coating my hair in age, weariness, fear. They come down down down and fill in the tracks with a coat of purest white.

For a little while, I can forget. For a little while, I pretend.

Sharpened Wood As Problem Solver

The door pounds again, bending under the strain. "What the hell is..."

Sarah is ash grey, eyes wide beneath her dreads. Overstrong sandalwood incense still makes me want to sneeze, but now I can smell something else underneath. Something stale copper.

"Missy said," Sarah's voice is a squeak, "she's becoming a sangui...doing some vampire thing with these hot college guys..." There is a scratching at the window, and I know we can't escape.

"Put your clothes back on, baby," I tell her, counting the hours until sunrise. I smash the wood furniture, making impromptu stakes.

Thank God for Ikea.

Post-Suicide Life

For a while after the attempt, everything was spectacular.

It was as if a sensory grime was vomited with the sleeping pills and charcoal, and left behind in the ER's biohazard bag. He drank in the sky's shifting shades of blue, the smell of grass and gasoline on suburban weekends. He even savored the oaty richness of generic cereal scraping down his throat.

He was discharged, but doctors warned that relapse was often subtle.

"People feel fine but don't notice the symptoms returning."

He wouldn't forget. He promised he would be back to see them -- when cereal was boring again.

Opening

"Are we supposed to be up here?"

The third attic stair squeaked before I answered my sister's whine.

"Mom is gone for the afternoon. I am bored and in charge until they get back. So, yes."

The attic was full of Grandmother's old stuff. Here there was a stack of yellowing magazines, there were some musty papers and old books. Under it all was the prize: Her old steamer trunk, blackened with age and oil.

"Bobby, I heard Grandma was a witch."

Grandma's name - Pandora Spyros - was written just above the latch. I ignored my sister and opened Grandmother's box.

Hidden

They let me into my parent's house. It's a beautiful day - outside air spring cool and clean, so the stench inside is so much worse.

My parents had got back from the movies. He was waiting for them. He had no reason, just the feel of metal through skin.

The couch is stained with their blood.

They took the bodies away, but not the blood. This time they'll catch him, they say. Sure.

I see the glint the detectives missed, see the knife under my father's chair. I see the glistening blade, and pretend the dark on it is rust.

Kilt

I stared at Tom, sweating in the humid heat. "Ach, lad, why are you wearing pants in this weather?"

Tom looked at his slacks. "I'm fine. And I don't look like a girl."

I almost hit him, but the breeze under my tartans kept me cool. "I canna wear these in Edinburgh anymore, lad. The Gulf Stream shuttin' down means Scotland's a bloody glacier." I swirled the kilt again, enjoying the air. "But Michigan..."

"Enough!" Tom yelled. Sweat dripped as he ripped off the trousers. "Just give me a damn skirt."

"Kilt," I said, laughing and walking off with his pants.

Lingua Fracas

"I do not like to speak Spanish in public," she said, hoping he and his bright, inquisitive eyes would just go away.

"Well, could I practice with you? I am having problems in my Spanish class."

Kate ("Katiana," her mother whispers in accented English) twirls a dyed blonde strand of her hair. She prays he has not heard her call home.

"No. I do not remember that much, anyway. I am sorry."

"Lo siento, tambien," he says, walking away.

That night, she hears Univision from her mother's television and cries. It is a melodramatic soap opera.

She understands every word.

Hunting

Harsh morning sunlight woke me in the field. I was beside the gnawed-on corpse of Vinnie. Bits of shredded clothes and shredded Vinnie slid off me when I stood up. Damn. Three weeks of undercover work ruined because I was hungry and couldn't remember wolfsbane.

I gave Vinnie's corpse a once-over, not expecting anything left. Chewed tendon, maybe, but not a... pre-paid cell phone. With an incoming call on it.

My smile scared the desk cop when he traced the call, when he gave me a name. Tonight, I will solve the case.

Tonight, I will hunt by moonlight.

Aw, Zombies

"Aw, hell. Zombies."

Professor Heath laughed from across the bar.

"No, they're whiskey sours."

He drank his, then poured more gunpowder into his shotgun shells. Nicole poured another round of whiskey, then passed out rounds for our pistols.

"I thought," she said, "Romero's zombie movies were a commentary on the mindless nature of modern American society."

"What, nihilism?" I snorted. "It's all mindless and will eat you in the end?"

The Professor stood and smiled.

"There is only one effective response to both nihilism and the undead." He took aim through the boards on the window and fired.

"Decisive action."

Generational Engine

The wrench flies from the engine, close enough that I taste flecks of rust. Grandfather yells, a balding series of spheres in the front seat. I already know I'm worthless, thanks. I wipe the grease onto my ruined shirt, he dabs a pressed handkerchief at his forehead.

The wrench and my hand slide back in. It - he won't identify it - must be held just so. The key cranks, washing the smell of exhaust and gasoline over me.

The car roars to life. He lumbers inside, shouting how he fixed the car.

The wrench smashes a beautiful music through the windshield.

Tales of Heroes

Cherry blossoms perfume the air, decorating it with the fall of their petals. I stand before her, my katana soiled with the blood of her enemies. Her rescued family is my wedding offering.

I have read the tales of heroes. I fashioned my armor, my habits, my life in imitation of them. I completed their trials, their feats. I am the greatest of them.

I smile at her. I have read the tales of heroes, and I know how this will end.

She turns, walking away under the cherry blossoms.

As in all the tales of heroes, a nightingale sings.

Oceans

In 2012, the whales told us they were intelligent.

Then they told us they were causing global warming.

My roommate giggled as the whale songs were translated into the details of the libertarian Federation of Ceteceans. He laughed harder as the whales revealed their ongoing plan.

Carbon dioxide was the first step. Next, they would free methane trapped at the ocean floor, spiking the temperature and turning the Earth into... well, the Water.

"That's horrible," I said.

"Don't you see the irony?" he asked. "They're libertarians. They don't believe in environmental impact statements!"

I thought I could smell salt water.

Hidden Relationships

"Cindy, this is Jason from work, and his wife Megan." Dan ushered the two into the kitchen, away from the noises of the party.

"Cindy," Megan said, "I saw your daughter today. She's so adorable!"

"Yes, Dan," Jason said, "She looked wonderful in that dress. Did you say you had a son, too? Where's he?"

Dan and Cindy glanced at each other, at the basement door, then to their guests.

"He's visiting his grandparents," Cindy said quickly. "Let's go join the others back in the den."

Neither Dan nor Cindy glanced at the door for the rest of the evening.

Family Recipe

"You didn't get the dressing right again, dear," he called from the table. In the kitchen, she clenched her eyes and hands and took what were supposed to be five deep breaths. She could hear him crunching the salad, despite his complaints.

She tried to sound pleasant and cheerful through clenched teeth. "Oh?"

"I don't think you got the mix of oil and vinegar quite right. Did you call my momma to ask how she makes it?"

"I followed her recipe. Dear."

"Well, you still didn't get it right. Again."

He gasped as she poured first the vinegar, then oil, then a powdery mix of herbs on his head.

"I think it's just right now."

Festival

The streets were as alive as downtown Marysville ever got. Jonah watched them eat funnelcakes, scream on cheap rides, and play the carnival games. The annual Olive Loaf Festival had not changed a bit. He remembered trying to explain it to Mary before he came home.

"Small towns, they find something - anything - they can call their own. Some reason to feel special."

Her raised eyebrow had spoken volumes of sarcasm.

Back there he had been a nobody. Now, the festival crowd laughed and swirled around him. Jonah held his picture of Mary and danced down the street with it, smiling.

Parasites

The church looked down at the ranch home in the next lot. "Excuse you."

The house blushed, the sounds of copulating echoing from inside. "Human infestation," it said. "It happens."

"Balderdash!" said the church, raising its voice above the moans from next door. "They are sent by God to afflict the wicked!"

"You're nuts!" said the house. The church scoffed, its humans raising their voices in praise and song.

When night came, a black cloud came close - bats flying back to their church steeple home. The house giggled to itself.

"I knew you had bats in your belfry," it said.

Impossible

He towered, skin like soggy matzo, hulking over the swarthy man; an oxycontin-fueled mass of rage.

"That's wrong! Count the ballots again!" he shouted into the night sky, shaking a meaty fist at the uncaring moon. "I have millions of listeners, agreeing with my every word! I am the voice of real America!" He pointed again at the swarthy swordsman leaning against the wall. "This will be the end of America! People like this Spaniard more than me? Inconceivable!"

"That word," the swarthy man said, "you keep saying it. I do not think it means what you think it means."

Recipe

One. Take one candlestick. Combine with the brain of your ex-lover at high speed. In the library.

Two. Wipe fingerprints from fixtures and door handles for thirty seconds.

Three. Use two cups of the victim's blood to write radical slogans for a religion you do not follow on the walls.

Four. Place body in bathtub filled with sulfuric acid. Allow to steep until soft..

Five. Knead C4 around support pillars of home. Place detonators.

Six. Exit, then detonate. Allow all ingredients to cook until fire and police departments arrive.

Seven. Watch TV anchors speculate about your identity.

Serves one.

Out of Gas

I go over the edge of the trench with the gas. It rolls in thick liquid clouds.

The enemy is surprised. Both of us are hampered by gas masks. My bayonet slices up, straps snap, and his mask falls away.

His eyes widen into owl eyes, pupils dilating from the poison. Snot and blood pour from his mouth and nose. He clutches his chest and gasps to a stop. His bowels release staining his trousers as he dies.

I breathe in through my mask's charcoal filters. I smell nothing.

I raise my rifle and shoot a stranger twenty feet away.

Sizing Your Returns

The vase twists and falls from his hand, spilling roses across the floor. She holds her mother's old suitcase over her chest, the nobby green 1970's plastic rough against her silk dress.

Her voice is flat: "I'm sorry. You were scheduled to return tomorrow."

His voice is an uncomfortable goiter stuck in his throat.

"Who?" he croaks.

She points at Robert's old VW bus pulling in the mansion drive.

"But..." he gestures at the building, her dress. "Him? He can't give you this. Were there not enough roses? Is the house too small?"

She sighs. "Bigger isn't always better, Tony."

Timing

Now.

PFC Fenti flinches, but there is no explosion. The driver glances at him, then watches the road again.

Now. Nothing.

Bullets fail to come streaking from the windows. Simmons lights a Camel - irony is cheap here - and blows smoke in Fenti's face.

Spielberg would consider that a cue; the insurgents do not.

Tense, boring minutes pass. A drip of sweat falls from Fenti's head onto his weapon.

Now.

No bullets. No IED. Nothing.

He says it: "Remember, it's not just a job..."

When the left side of the hummer goes in flame and shrapnel, it's almost a relief.

Now.

Fuck Cancer

She adjusts herself on the sheet. The technician straps her in and steps out of the room. The table slides her towards the scanner's large ominous doughnut.

"Hold your breath," the computerized voice says. A whir, then: "Breathe."

They saw it first on the x-ray, the little dot now an invading force. "Hold your breath." Pause. "Breathe."

It colonized one lung, lymph nodes, spleen. "Hold your breath. Breathe."

This is what it must feel like to be Iraq, she imagines. "Hold your breath." Her bones ache with cellular Abu Gharibs and Basras. How much has fallen?

"Breathe."

"Hold your breath."

Kilt II

"I kilt my Paw."

For a moment, I expected the boy to present a bear foot dressed in Highland tartan. Instead, he held out a bloodied shovel.

"I kilt my Paw with this'n shovel."

Cool filtered air blew into my isolation suit. I patted the boy's matted hair with a gloved hand. "Where's your mother, son? Do you have any brothers or sisters?"

The boy pointed to the locked root cellar. We both heard undead moans.

"Paw bit Maw and Sissy," the boy said.

I drew my pistol. The boy stopped me with a hand, raised his shovel, and went in.

Lobster

Ron was trying to avoid puking.

"Relax, Ronster!" Matt held the lobster by its tail. The animal writhed, and Ron imagined that it knew about the pot boiling on the cabin's stove.

"God, but it'll scream," Ron said. "I've heard that they scream." Trips with Matt always ended up this way - Matt enjoying being cruel to some animal, and enjoying Ron's discomfort almost as much.

"It's just steam coming out of the -" A knock at the door interrupted Matt. "I'm not waiting for you, asshat."

Ron fled the kitchen and went to the cabin's door. The ranger looked serious.

"You boys been up here long?"

"Just got here today, sir. What's wrong?"

"I didn't know anyone was up here. The well water's been contaminated by some kind of chemical spill from a government lab. They won't tell me anything more than... you boys haven't drank any, have you?"

"No, just-" Ron's words were drowned out by the scream of the lobster.

Then by the rattle of a pot hitting the floor and Matt's scream.

The next scream was much louder. It was not from Matt. It sounded eerily like steam escaping from a carapace.

Ron and the ranger ran.

Hospitality

"There, grandpa," Mike said, his young hand releasing the wood tile. "I spelled PIT. How many points is that?"

Grandfather looked at the board. "I think it's ten."

"Did you play this game a lot with grandma before she died?"

"Yes. We played most nights." Grandfather put his tiles down on the board.

"Hospital."

The boy frowned and hummed, then his face lit up as he put down his letters. "Hospitality," he said.

"Congratulations," Grandfather said. "You win!"

As they left the room, they left behind the game board.

There, for a little while, hospitality was spelled with two e's.

Waiting Room

The machine goes ping and she stifles a laugh. They loved that movie.

His hands are cold in hers, so she is not surprised when the rhythmic ping changes to a whine, then to the chaos of nurses and doctors performing a full code. She allows herself to be ushered out to the sterile comfort of the waiting room.

Couples fight silently overhead, the trash tv thankfully muted. Her fingers caress the worn gold of her ring. She wonders if she will wear it once he has gone.

She sees the doctor in the doorway, and stands to meet him.

Eating Preferences

"These doughnuts are awesome, Mrs. Sprat," Amanda said through her glaze-covered lips. "I can barely help myself from just eating all of them."

"It's just my way of saying merry Christmas to the office," Mrs. Sprat replied. "Do you think everyone likes them?"

Amanda waved at the nearly-empty boxes. "Of course they do! They're almost all gone! Did your husband take some to his office?"

"Oh, no. Jack's office is all on Atkins or South Beach."

Amanda grinned, waving the partially eaten pastry at her co-worker. "We'll need to here, too, if you keep bringing in so many good things to eat. I'm going to put on five pounds today, I'm sure of it."

Mrs. Sprat smiled. "We'll have quite a feast at the office's holiday party."

Amanda paused, and tilted her head to the side. "I didn't think Mark had decided on a final menu yet."

Mrs. Sprat smiled even wider. "I'm sure it'll be excellent. I hope to see you there."

Amanda smiled again. "Sure! And will Jack be there?"

"No," Mrs. Sprat replied, "but I'm sure he'll be just as well fed at his own office party."

Hills and Valleys

Look, I don't know why I'm here. Even if you could hear me, the ventilator's too damn loud. You would think that a nice hospital like this one would have a newer model. Maybe it's because Medicaid's paying for all this. I dunno.

Robert's doing well. He's responding to therapy. You wouldn't like his therapist; I'm not sure I do. But it's working. They tell me it's because he's still young. He's young enough that we - his therapist and I, not you, of course - can work to undo the damage. All the crap you did to him while I was overseas.

Still, I wouldn't have known to take him if you hadn't ended up here.

The lines on the monitors always remind me of little mountain ranges. Up and down, like back home. Yes, my home, thanks for reminding me again. I know, I know, you were born out in Kansas, where it's flat. Right. You always complained about the mountains, about having to walk up and down those hills. Robert asked if he could visit, but they won't let kids on the ICU here. You had to go and overdose in some backwards place, somewhere that hadn't heard of letting kids get closure.

Then again, maybe he's had enough closure.

Anyway, it's a long drive up here. I'm not sure I'll be back either. I need some closure too.

Still, I shouldn't be rude. Here, let me fix the view for you.

You always preferred flat plains to mountains.

Why?

Bob the Zombie looked over at his friend Sara. She was busy scooping the brains out of a young man's head. Bob had the woman's date half out of the car.

"Sara," Bob said (although it sounded like "Gwddaaarrrgngg", because, well, zombies), "why are we eating brains?"

"MmmmNmphmmm," Sara said (because, well, she had her mouth full of dura mater).

"I'm not sure I want to eat this brain," Bob said, handing the woman to Sara.

"Don't you like the taste?" Sara asked. (She had swallowed.)

Bob shrugged. "It's okay, I guess. I guess I'd just rather have a nice pepperoni pizza."

Sara stuck out the remains of her tongue. "Eww. I'm a vegetarian."

They both let this moment pass in a short silence before Sara ripped the woman's nose off with her teeth.

"Seriously, Sara," Bob said. "I don't want to eat brains anymore."

"You have to," she said. "You're a zombie."

"But-"

"You don't have to like it, Bob. Zombies eat brains. It's one of those things you just have to do after you die." Sara gave the woman's ear a few thoughtful chews.

"It's de rigor."

Morning

You're standing outside, watching the sun rise. It's early enough that the neighborhood hasn't started to wake; only a few birds sing welcome. I join you, coming through the patio door in time to see you shiver, slightly, in the cool air. From behind I wrap a blanket around your shoulders, my arms around your sides. Our breath steams in intricate clouds as we watch the sun rise.

The clouds will come soon. The cars, the smog. Cell phones and business appointments. Perhaps we will fight - today, another day. It will come. Arguments and recriminations, changing lives and differing goals. One day, we will look back and wonder how we became so far apart when we were so close.

But now. Now, you shiver, and I hold you close. Now, it is just you and I, and the morning sun.

And for now, it is enough.

Protest

"Oh, hi," he said, moving his sign to the side so he could see her a little bit better. "It's been a while, yeah?"

She flushed, and smiled so widely that his heart was lifted up with the corners of her mouth. "Too long," she said. "Are you here for the demonstration?"

Even if he could have helped it, he wouldn't have stopped his mind from skipping over the fights, the arguments, the breakup. It skipped and danced right back to the fun times, the nights spent together laughing, naked or clothed. His memories kept skipping to the days where he could be held enraptured by the soft color of her hair, by its surprising robustness. The days where the sighs were contentment, not exasperation. The days, he realized, he wanted back again.

She repeated the question, louder over the gathering crowd of people. "Are you here for the demonstration?"

Smiling, he held out the big "YES" sign. "Yeah, would you like to get coffee after...?"

His tongue dried in his mouth as she slowly held out the "NO" sign from behind her back.

Meeting Santa

"I don't understand why we bother," he groused, dodging yet another overloaded shopper careening past. The line moved forward a step. The three of them - he, his wife, and son - moved together. Step.

His wife nudged him into silence, her voice pitched so the boy couldn't hear it over the piped-in carols. "We do it for him."

"But it's not real," he said, waving his hand at the front of the line. The boy's gaze was still fixed there, entranced by costumed performers and faux mall elves. "It's all just a fantasy. It's just something in his head."

His wife turned full towards him, hands on hips. "Lots of things are true just because someone believes in them."

"Like what?"

"Like our marriage."

He turned away from her cold eyes, her hard face. He turned back towards the glittering plastic snow, towards the cracked plaster and fading candy cane gates of the model North Pole.

The line moved forward a step.

"We do it for him," his wife said. "We do it for him."

Voice

Like jasmine, nighttime soft and delicate, heard in the
    sudden pause of a dozen conversations.
Like curry, seasoning small talk into sublime soul sharing.
Like molasses, soft and comforting, though we're "just friends".
Like pure summer dew, innocent and clear kisses.
Like sugar, delicious and excruciatingly sweet.
Like butter, melting words enhancing our flavor.
Like yellow sliced cheese, once delightful, now blasÃ©.
Like jalapeno, ferocious heat cursing stupid infidelities.
Like ice, a no-taste defined by cold, the absence of heat
Like copper, metallic aftertaste lingering long
    after the real thing is gone.
Like whiskey, hateful burning but never, ever enough.

Leaving

The sheet fell across his face, the white cotton cutting a line parallel to the hot sunbeam. Still, it took him a moment - three breaths filtered by the fabric - before he began to stir. He raised up on his elbows, and watched the denim slide up her legs.

"Hey."

She glanced back at him, then pulled the sweat-top over her head. The cellophane crinkled as she picked up the pack of cigarettes, lighting one.

She blew smoke in his face. "Good to know you're such an intellectual genius in the morning."

"You don't have to go yet, babe. Checkout's not until noon."

She took another deep breath, then blew smoke into the cheap light fixture. She stood up, stepped to the dresser. Her purse went onto her shoulder, her ring onto her finger. She looked back at him, and despite the sheet, he felt naked under her eyes.

She rubbed the ring around and around her finger while she spoke. "I have to leave, because if I don't, I will."

She kissed him once more, on the forehead like a favored child, then turned to go home from her business trip.

Cold

We broke up long distance. She crushed my heart by e-mail.

It wasn't her fault. Not really. We were just separated temporarily for her job. Six months, then she'd be back. We'd be back, together. It was a trial separation, for fiscal reasons.

She e-mailed because she was too sick to be understood over the phone. I wanted to drive there, to simmer the chicken soup and boil the tea, to wrap the blanket around her. She always needed me to take care of her.

Even though I have the uber bug from hell, she wrote, I finally realized I can make my own damn soup.

The next paragraph told me she was going overseas, teaching English to willing Vietnamese children. Her flight left in a week, and she wouldn't be coming back to our home. I couldn't fill the hole in my stomach with rum, whisky, vodka. I couldn't pretend that she was just around the corner when she was in a different day.

When I started sneezing and my temperature spiked, I smiled. I left the windows open and kept my hair wet. I threw the chicken noodle soup out for the insane tree-rat squirrels, and walked around without my shoes.

The fever ripped through me, hot and cold waves of sweat soaking the couch, and I cried with the joy of having a little something of hers back with me again.

ABOUT THE AUTHOR

Steven Saus injects people with radioactivity as his day job, but only to serve the forces of good. He tries to tell lies that are absolutely true.

His work has also appeared in print in several anthologies and magazines both online and off. You can find them all at stevensaus.com, and read his blog at ideatrash.net.

www.ingramcontent.com/pod-product-compliance
Lightning Source LLC
Chambersburg PA
CBHW071203130626
46555CB00004B/1567

* 9 7 8 0 9 8 4 0 0 6 5 2 6 *